Rockets

HAUNTED MOUSE

Magenta and the Ghost School

Dee Shulman

A & C Black • London

Rockets series:

CROOK CATCHERS - Karen Wallace & Judy Brown

HAUNTED MOUSE - Dee Shulman

LITTLE T - Frank Rodgers

MOTLEY'S CREW - Margaret Ryan & Margaret Chamberlain

MR CROC - Frank Rodgers

MRS MAGIC - Wendy Smith

MY FUNNY FAMILY - Colin West

ROVER - Chris Powling & Scoular Anderson

SILLY SAUSAGE - Michaela Morgan & Dee Shulman

WIZARD'S BOY - Scoular Anderson

First paperback edition 2002
First published 2002 in hardback by A & C Black (Publishers) Ltd
37 Soho Square, London W1D 3QZ

Text and illustrations copyright © 2002 Dee Shulman

The right of Dee Shulman to be identified as author
and illustrator of this work has been asserted by her
in accordance with the Copyright, Designs and Patents Act 1988.

ISBN 0-7136-5979-3

A CIP catalogue record for this book is available
from the British Library.

Printed and bound by G. Z. Printek, Bilbao, Spain.

Chapter One

'Coooeee little ghosts!' called Magenta Mouse. 'It's time for your ghostly gummy sweety treat!'

From every corner of the Haunted House
ghost children came gliding...

WHOOSH!

WHOOSH!

'Right ghostlings,' said Magenta, holding out the basket of sweets, 'there's enough for two sweets each.'

'Hey, Hey, Hey!' scolded Magenta. 'You need to learn some manners! How many sweets have you got there Dora?'

Dora held out her hand.

Well?

Don't know...

Of course you do – now put three back!

Dora began to cry.

What's
three?

Magenta couldn't believe her ears. 'Dora, are you telling me that you can't count?'

Dora started to wail.

What's
Counting?

Magenta looked around. 'Don't any of you know how to count?'

All the little ghosts blinked at her blankly.

'I know how to... haunt...' said little Bozo desperately.

The ghostlings' lips wobbled.

9

Chapter Two

Magenta knew she had to do something. So she called a house meeting.

She was just about to start talking when
Sir Boris, the grumpiest of the ghosts,
started hammering his fist on the table.

Magenta—you've really
gone too far this time!
Look what you've done
to our little
ghostlings—

Sir Boris, these ghostlings—

'Don't interrupt me, Mouse,
I haven't finished.
Now – where was I?
Yes – look at them
blubbering all
over the place –
they've soaked
my best suit.'

Godfrey and Loretta complained.

'Exactly,' agreed Felix. 'Before *you* decided it was *treat* time, they were lying around as quiet as graves.'

Magenta squeaked crossly. 'These little ghosts are lying around quiet as graves when they should be bright, perky and learning things! In fact, they should be... at **SCHOOL!**'

'You're about to find out!' said Magenta
decisively.

Chapter Three

A few days later all the
little ghostlings were gliding
in a lovely, smart line
through the gates of
their new school.

15

A bell sounded, and their new teacher, Miss Dimble, led them into their classroom.

Sukie loved learning about numbers.

Billy liked writing
his name.

And all the ghosts liked painting!

SPLOSH!

SPLISH!

SPLASH!

Chapter Four

The trouble began in P.E.

Miss Dimble divided the class into two teams.

She told them how
they could score goals
by throwing the ball
through the hoop.

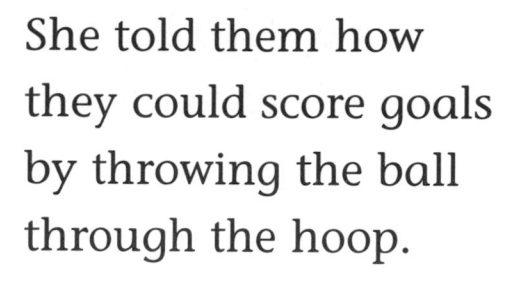

Easy!

All the children
were excited.

Can we
start?

It wasn't long before Sukie, Freddie and Dora had scored thirty goals each.

20

The human children weren't happy.

So then the ghost children weren't happy.

By dinner time the ghostlings were so tired of being called cheats that they decided to spend playtime as far away from the human children as possible.

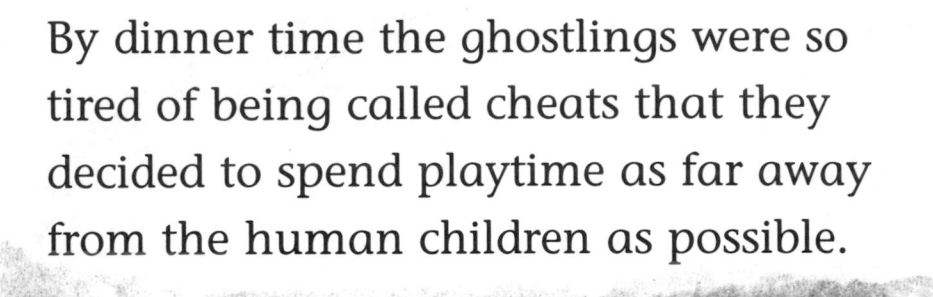

But the playground was so far down, they didn't hear the bell for afternoon school.

Miss Dimble had to come out and find them...

...she was very cross indeed.

Will you come down from there at once!

Chapter Five

When the ghostlings had all floated down from the roof, Miss Dimble told the class some exciting news.

'Now then children, I want you all to stand on the stage for our opening song.'

The children did their best...

Some got there in the end...

But some didn't...

Then Miss Dimble started
playing the piano for the
lovely song.

Everybody started to sing,
especially the ghostlings,
who loved singing.

Unfortunately, Miss Dimble and the human children had never heard singing quite like it before.

Even the school hall wasn't used to such a sound.

SCREECH

So Miss Dimble stopped playing the piano and screamed.

STOP SCREECHING AT ONCE!

The ghost children were heart broken.

WAILLL

HOWLLL

But we love singing!

Boo Hoo!

Boo Hoo!

Chapter Six

Magenta was just on her way to collect her little ghostlings from their first day at school when they nearly knocked her over.

Ghostlings! Why aren't you in school?

We're **never** going back!

But by the time Magenta got to the school, Miss Dimble was just leaving.

Magenta looked around. All the classrooms were empty.

How could she go home and face everyone?

So Magenta went and sat in the ghostling's classroom to have a little think.

Magenta sat there thinking so long that she didn't notice it getting dark.

Neither did she notice a shadowy figure glide sadly through the door and sit down at the teacher's desk.

But she did notice the noise when it began...

WAILLL! If only I had some children to teach! All my little pupils have grown up and gone away! Booooo Hoooo!

41

Magenta couldn't believe her ears.

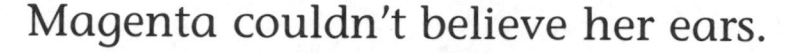

Excuse me... did you just wail that you want some children to teach?

I come every night, and hope and wait... sniff

'Can you just wait for a few minutes more?' squeaked Magenta heading for the door.

I have waited forty years – what's a few more minutes?

Chapter Seven

In no time at all Magenta's ghostlings were getting a lovely history lesson...

Then they had a great game of plopball.

45

After their midnight feast, they all went on a little Geography trip...

47

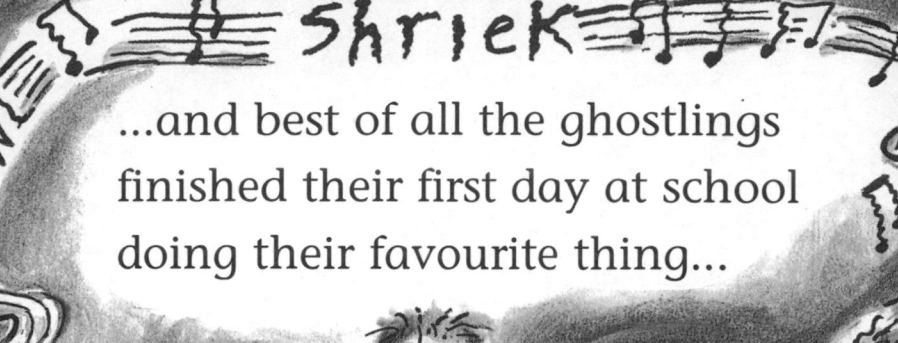

...and best of all the ghostlings finished their first day at school doing their favourite thing...